AF582460

DISARRAYED

Disarrayed
Edited & Compiled by
Binta Elsa Biju

Paperback Edition

First published in India in 2023 by

Inkfeathers Publishing
Vivek Vihar, New Delhi 110095
www.inkfeathers.com

ISBN 978-81-19483-74-7

Copyrights owned by authors of each published write-up within this book.

All rights reserved. No part of this book may be reproduced, lent, resold, or transmitted in any form or by any means, electronic or mechanical, including photocopying, recording, or by any other information storage and retrieval system, without permission in writing from the publisher and the copyright owner.

DISARRAYED

Edited & Compiled by

Binta Elsa Biju

Inkfeathers Publishing
www.inkfeathers.com

Disclaimer

The anthology "Disarrayed" is a collection of 2 articles, 5 short stories and 31 poems written by 29 authors who belong to different parts of the world.

Unless otherwise indicated, all the names, characters, objects, businesses, places, events, incidents—whether physical/non-physical, real/unreal, tangible/ intangible in whatsoever description used in this book are either the product of the author's imagination or used in a fictitious manner. Any resemblance to actual persons, objects, entities, living or dead, or actual events is purely coincidental.

The contents published in this book are solely owned by their respective authors and are in no way intended to hurt anyone's religious, political, spiritual, brand, personal or fanatic beliefs and/or faith, whatsoever. In case, any sort of plagiarism is detected in the contents within this anthology or in case of any complaints, grievances, or objections, neither the anthology editor nor the publisher is to be held responsible.

Curated with the writings of

Anna Reji, Asad Chaugule, Bhavika Gupta, Reeba John,
Anju Elizabeth Kurien, Khushi Shukla, Alen Tharakan,
Rhythmi Rosa. S, Jagruthi Kommuri, Srishti Kala, Hema S,
Srishti Karkara, Praneel Dev, Susmin Eapen, Divvya Gupta,
Amiteshwar Singh, Bhuvi Gupta, Juwel Zacharia,
Gauri Agarwal, Ananya Singh, Keertika Shivee, Halo Golwin,
Varnika Sasi Magesh, Swastika Bhattacharyya, Kai Jennings,
Bhakti Barad, Srishti Sareen, Sanay Shah, Binta Elsa Biju

Contents

Short Stories

Articles

Meet the Editor

Binta Elsa Biju

"When life gives you lemons, make orange juice and leave the world wondering how you did it".

The editor's encounter with the quote has a seminal influence in this work of art. Whenever get struck by the adversities of life, always strive to find the silver lining in every situation. Binta firmly believes that hard work beats talent and the world is for those, who never give up. Everything will fall in place one day and we must learn to celebrate each life situation with the thought, "The best is yet to be".

Binta Elsa Biju is a budding editor from Thiruvalla, Kerala with a passion for the written word. A post graduate of English Language and Literature from Mar Ivanios College, Thiruvananthapuram, she is currently pursuing a Bachelor's Degree in Education. She is an ardent lover of literature, believing it as one of the ideal ways to explore and address the complexities of human psyche. This anthology "Disarrayed" is her maiden attempt as an editor, even though she has already made her presence felt as a writer through a few anthologies.

She is particularly interested in the theme of fragmentation, hoping that this anthology will resonate with readers, who are looking for a reflection of their own fragmented selves. She finds happiness in engaging herself in the mesmerizing world of letters and she is truly excited to continue her new role as an editor, to help bringing new voices to the literary world.

Binta is a passionate soul, eagerly wishing to be a proponent of fruitful thoughts and actions in the journey towards her dreams.

Editor's Note

In a world that is increasingly chaotic and fragmented, it is of no wonder that our thoughts and emotions can feel the same way. Our thoughts can race, our emotions can fluctuate, and we can feel like, we are constantly on the verge of losing control.

This anthology entitled "Disarrayed" is a collection of works that reflect this experience of uncoupled as well as fragmented thoughts and emotions. The writers have given voice to the chaos and confusion that we all feel at times. One quote that stands out in particular is from the eminent writer Ernest Hemingway: "The world breaks everyone, and afterward, some are strong at the broken places." This quote perfectly captures the sense of disarray that permeates the anthology.

Even though we are facing trials and tribulations in this unrelenting journey and getting puzzled by our life situations, we are capable enough to encounter them. There is a strength that helps us to maintain an order in disorder. It is okay to feel fragmented and uncoupled. It is okay to not have answers for all the questions that trouble us. In fact, it is often in these moments of disarray that we learn the most about ourselves.

This anthology primarily aims at revealing a different perception of the conglomeration of varied emotions and thoughts. It is possible to find beauty in chaos and coherence in incoherence.

Hope you will find this as an engrossing and thought-provoking collection, and I am sure that it will help you to see yourself in a new light.

Happy Reading.

Binta Elsa Biju

Editor

If Not I Read

Anna Reji

If not I read,
I would have restrained
Myself from scribbling
These letters…

If not I read,
I would have eulogized
An idle woman as
A divine spirit…

If not I read,
I would have continued to
Believe that a timid woman
Looks enticing to men…

If not I read,
I would have still relied
On my father to fetch those bags to
The bus stop...

What is Failure?

Praneel Dev

What is failure, how do you comprehend it?
Is it climbing a mountainous goal, only to
Drop you into a crevice?
Or is it a slip at shooting for the stars and
Then failing to answer, "How did I miss"?

What is failure, can you commend it?
Do you sit down with your heart out and accept it?
Or do you lash out with your fangs out and aggress it?
What is failure, how does it hit you?
Is it a bold black blank in one's sound mind?
Or is it a heartless hole you find in your chest?

What is failure, do you accept it?
Do you greet it as an unwelcomed guest?
Or do you meet it like a long-lost friend after a test?
What is failure is it really useful?
Is it a necessary stepping-stone to attain success?
Or is it just a harbinger of utter mess?

What is failure, how do you amend it?
Do you ignore it and run away in vain?
Or do you conquer it and use it for gain?
What is failure, should we fear its name?
Should we feebly fall as pebbles in an abyss?
Or should we rise as champions destined for greatness?

What is failure, but a stepping stone to success?
Is it a place to review, reason and to assess?
Or is it a small hiccup, where we learn courage from distress?

Fire-Stricken Cotton Heart

Rhythmi Rosa S

Cotton-hearted human nature
Gets fire -stricken by the worldly pressure,
Leads to mankind's fissure,
For a bleak future!

This rage is an alarming danger,
As time knows to intensify its effect.
Make an effort to control 'wrath',
To gift your world a tranquil future.

Pain

Amiteshwar Singh

Broken and tired after being a slave
Living in hell...
Yes, I feel the pain.
Existing but tethered inside this dark fortress,
Respiring every second...
Yes, I feel the pain.

I feel vexation just with the very sight of you,
While saying this...
Yes, I feel the pain.

Killed your heart, ignited your soul,
And now bearing your hatred...
Yes, I feel the pain.

Standing beside a grave with a sobbing heart,
Unable to cry…
Yes, I feel the pain.

Exploited by fate in order to meet my traitors again,
Calling for help...
Yes, I feel the pain.

Questing the Gods for decades,
Finding only devils...
Yes, I feel the pain.

Having worn a poker face
And faking a smile...
Yes, I feel the pain.

Driving towards the gates assuming it as heaven,
But finding another hell...
Yes, I feel the pain.

Get Up & Rise!

Asad Chaugule

Let the world know your desires,
Let everyone know you are on fire.
Let's shut the lost sagas of the past,
Let's write dreams, forever which will last.

Exhausted of being under the proletariat rulers,
Disgusted of being a languid follower,
It's the time to concoct your own regime,
It's time to be the victory's sovereign.

Get on the battlefield with your gallant shield,
To the calumny of people, do not pay heed.
Keep thy qualms in the grave,
Get up! Rise and be brave!

Fight your presage, grapple your angst,
Show them that your actions are earnest.
Universe will shine with your winning glare,
Trumpet of your triumph will be heard everywhere.

It Does Get Better

Praneel Dev

To the broken child hidden beneath
With tearful dreams and an empty sheath,
To the broken heart with holes plenty and
To the downtrodden boy with sadness hefty,

To the emotional wreck of years back,
To the manipulated freak with no cut slack.
To the sad, soft boy with a temper short,
To the bed sheet convict thinking of mort.

On the flip side of hopes and dreams,
To the boy whose sorrow flowed in streams.
To the child who feared looking up straight,
To the ones whose strings were pulled by hate.

To the terrible troubled terrified youth,
Too afraid to smile and face the truth.
To the misguided fractured jaded boy and
To the shattered mosaic devoid of joy.

To the boy with a leftover birthday cake,
To the ones whose invite no one would take.
To the child whose laughter ruffled many,
To the ones whose shoulders bowed,
Neck bent and not worth a penny.

Four words, one hope in red dripped letters,
Go on; go forth, 'it does get better'.

Life

Alen Tharakan

Bringer of good news,
Fountain of hope,
Not at all a cakewalk,
Sometimes boorish;
Desolate and despairing,
'Angel of Light',
Also known by the infamous
Sobriquet- 'Prince of Darkness'.
Multifaceted experiences
Offer numerous reasons to
Still love life.
Finding meaning and
Striving till death.
"Live life with no qualms",
A finding to be shared.

Will everything change?

Swastika Bhattacharyya

Is there light at the end of every tunnel?
That will lead me to a virtuous path.
Is there love at the end of every story?
That will make me perceive your credence.
Is there trust after every delusion?
That will bind an emotion.
Is there a way out of all the difficulties?
That will clarify all of my doubts.
Is there always a happy ending?
That I won't refer as a feign.

Is there a way to break the spell of love?
That is making me weaker evermore.
Millions of years passed in vain,
Is there anything left to gain?
Is there still an answer for every question?
That's veiled deep inside your heart.
Will you give an opportunity to rectify all my mistakes?
Is there life after love?
Will everything change?

The Broken Wings

Susmin Eapen

I always dreamt of flying high,
But one of my wings never let me fly.
The bleeding wing of mine
Was always a reason to whine.
I ought to reach the landscape of happiness,
Yet I landed in a desert of slothfulness.
Agony ruled over my soul
With no intention to console.
Time flew, wind blew,
That dream of mine never became true.

Hues of Life

Anju Elizabeth Kurien

Silver lining was not found,
Foiled up in silver, crushed and
Flickered as filtered through;
Smithered as it rushed through.

Stained blood red glass
Held me whole
Embittered, savoured untauglich
Traced the path to the depths of darkness!

No stars left
Painted my palette blue,
Life, a monochromic painting
With shades of blue.

The tree bled red,
Others bled white.
No hues of life is in place,
The morning dews wept.

Swelled up with unshed tears,
A tinge of red remained to mark the wound.
Dropped eyelids were
Powerless to bloom.

Wrapped up stardust
Inhaled by the warm hole,
Lifted to the twin,
Stretched my cells till they wore.

Black holes in my soul
Inhaled the universe,
No light escaped.
No holes concealed.

So deep were they.
There was still room for void,
Ready enough to engulf
The shades of blue.

The prism of dews and
The darkest secrets of black holes,
Both held mysteries
To be unfolded.

Washed ashore
Those shells of pearls, which
Once knew the depth of blue,
Now left the depth, hide under hues of grains.

If the Moon Could Talk Back

Varnika Sasi Magesh

If the moon could talk back,
She'd talk about how lonely she feels.
Despite all eyes looking at her and
The poems exalting her;
Despite her being the solace for man
In agony, dismay and distress,
Obviously oblivious to the multitude of
Hearts she heal,
For the millions of stars,
She has always been there.
But all that she could see is her lack of finesse.

She always reflected the light of the sun,
Never been herself, even though she's in a crowd of
Eight giant balls and umpteen smaller ones.
Though her neighbour is full of life,
She's never known to live on her own.

But yes, in the race of uniqueness and
Beauty, she's won.
For there are a million stars,
But she's the matchless one.

In the darkest of nights, she's been the usher.
Just has to find her way and to herself discover
That she's all above and more than what she could surmise,
That she just has to look at herself through my eyes.
Oh, my moon! Will you ever deem yourself worthy?
You being the only nightly emissary,
Will you ever show yourself mercy?

Note to Self

Khushi Shukla

My heart's hurt,
Eyelids about to shut,
Hair's messed mind's tired,
Spirits come spirits go,
Leaving me to deal with the woe,
When a voice buried deep,
Judders me to listen in,
That,
There will be light,
And there will gloom,
But let none ruffle you,
Let nothing unnerve you.

Sky's the limit,

No more no less,

Set your marvels tall,

Keep them fixed,

Chase them high,

Let no soul stop you,

Go on till you pursue.

Let's meet,

Beneath the orange burnt skies,

Share our laughs,

Share our cries,

Hold hands,

Attain our zenith,

Till we both satisfy.

Nightmares

Bhuvi Gupta

What is a nightmare?
A dream gone wrong?
Pretty little monsters?
Or a night stretched long?

Haunting me throughout the day,
Whispering in the dead of night.
They never let go,
Always holding me tight.

Mine aren't demons,
Nor are they zombies.
Hurtful words of my loving family
Are what that take my soul piece by piece.

In Search of Myself

Juwel Zacharia

In a world of strangers
With unfamiliar tongues and faces,
I sought to find myself,
To discover where my future embraces.

Lost in indecision,
Perplexed by the opinions of others,
I decided to be true to myself,
To find my path and my colours.

Leaving behind what I loved,
Making hard choices all along the way,
I know, I'm struggling hard,
To stay strong and to live another day.

This battle is for me alone,
And though it's tough, I'll persevere,
To ensure that I can keep thriving,
To cherish the life I have.

Changes

Ananya Singh

Our bodies were growing old;
Intellect was unripe and had yet to be moulded.

We were sent away from home;
to make a path of our own.

I sat in the car thinking about freedom;
not knowing it was just my phantasm.

A new city, new faces and a new me;
excited to face it altogether as 'we'.

Goodbyes were difficult;
But the joy of liberty felt great to exult.

Days had passed and life went upside down;
Now, every day we used to frown.

Our castle of dreams was bulldozed;
and the bricks of reality lay there-all exposed.

The bricks were too heavy to lift;
The mind and the heart were always in a rift.

It was hard to distinguish between a friend and a flatterer;
as everyone was striving to become the topper.

The pain of homesickness was unbearable;
And this disease was incurable.

Adulting came along with anxiety and stress;
Now, everything we had tried to do felt less.

After all, only our bodies were growing old;
But intellect, still unripe and had yet to be moulded.

Darkness is an Old Friend

Bhavika Gupta

Darkness is an old friend,
It keeps me company at night.
It ensures that I'm never alone and
It never leaves my sight.
It whispers to me,
It smirks and judges me.
It holds my head in its soothing arms,
Whenever I feel like I am drowning.

I drown in the depths of
The silence of darkness!
I am all alone and completely numb.
Its comments always hit the mark and
I will never be good enough as it is.
The darkness slowly lulls me to sleep,
Its stillness wraps around me like a blanket.
It holds me close and tight enough,
With promises of treating me the best.

The Girl in Pajamas

Bhakti Barad

This is a story about a girl in pajamas.
Cranky little thing in her pool,
She's surrounded by the nauseous scent of alcohol
Painted nails, which
She curls up and
Its fall is always in mid-October.
Her cheeks, dryer than all the maple leaves,
All her friends are lying against the grass with
Their hands holding in the car's back seat,
She sits in the middle, playing music for them.
Feels just like a movie when
They kiss in the end.

Girl in pajamas is in her own wonderland,
Sits with one numbed leg in a baseball T-shirt and
Screaming at her phone all the time!
She can't escape this facade of a room.
Coincidentally, it's also painted in blue,
The blue coffee mug sits idle like her.
She doesn't know all the pretty words,
The pretty boys or the pretty girls,

She doesn't know how to feel love;
Only knows to feel the pain that
Goes above her throat, her hair and
Her skin that's fair.

Jealous all the time,
A girl who only bites, a girl who laughs at jokes,
A girl who chokes on her words,
A girl who is afraid of the world,
Girl in pajamas is a messy girl,
Egocentric mind stalker having emotionless pricks…
She plays all tricks, then
Shuts herself in a locker!
Calls herself an alien in a spaceship!
What kind of a girl she is?
Is it her fault that she's all alone?

Paradox

Srishti Kala

What makes what happens,
Happen!
Is it the happening...! Or the
Vision that happens upon it!
A snowflake never melts,
A star never falls
Without being known by the 'Eye' that makes them true.

But no eye gazes upon the
Abyss of my heart,
The sparks that emanate
From my smile brighten no screen.
And yet the truth of them is
More sublime than the stars
And the sun,
So what makes what happens, happen!

The eye that witnesses,
The heart that feels,
Or what happens...
Just happens...!

Meaningful Life

Divvya Gupta

Command the stammering actuality,
Aim to dwell with solidarity.
Gain immunity by growth
And attain balance.
Respect guidance; practice patience.

Be kind and sacrificing.
Stop accusing to
Start achieving.
Put back pride with belief,
Show oneness in moments of grief.

Make each day count,
Let all sincere efforts account.
Time wasted is gone,
Focus and make the novel
Contents distinct and engrossing!

Arrest the flaws of desire,
Form an empire before you retire.
Settle for nothing less than
The real value…
Set goals, achieve, and continue.

Parallel Lines

Jagruti Kommuri

Same direction; side by side,
Every step, a roller coaster ride.
We were once happy and satisfied,
But along the way, proximity grew wide.

The journey was all that mattered,
None of us thought we might get shattered.
This strange path leads us 'nowhere',
Our love was true but fate wasn't fair.

Now living with pain and skipped heartbeats,
Like a story that is left incomplete.
A question we tried hard to defeat,
How can two parallel lines ever meet?

Destroyed

Keertika Shivee

If light is what light seems to be,
Why are shadows then more comforting?
How can in darkness passion stirs,
Why are kisses meant for lost being?

If hope is what has kept life going,
Why do we feel most alive in suffering?
How come breathing while crying seems satisfying?
Why does broken heart keep strengthening?

If reality is what defines someone,
How come illusion gives more meanings?
Why do people believe in always dreaming?
Why do people chase feelings?

If words are used to create bonds,
How come they shatter someone's heart?
How come people use it to destroy lives?
Why do the real ones always stay silent?

If lives were meant to be gift from the universe,
How come some of us live it as a curse?
How come with every turn they are always hurt?
Why is the end more comforting than birth?

If smiles were what spread joy,
A lot would have smiled when they saw themselves in eyes,
A lot less had been destroyed,
Someone like me, would have survived.

Twilight of Dreams

Praneel Dev

The world looks sober; colourless somehow,
Devoid of that childish glint in everything 'wow',
The child has grown up but his fervour on leave,
His heart aches for the long-gone naive.

By the light at the end of the tunnel,
He sees nothing but a grand funnel,
That sieves all those golden joys
Into bottles shaped like children's toys.

He accepts his solitude and rejection.
From the embrace of childish celebration,
A wry smile shows in tearful reams.
At last, he drifts off in the twilight of his dreams.

The Weird Being

Gauri Agarwal

Isn't it weird that I want to stand out
In a strange crowd?
But at the same time,
I want to hide from those eyes.
The eyes that judge me,
The eyes that think they know me
Like they know what is in my head,
Like some psychic lad.

Isn't it weird that I want to look pretty
To people I won't see, when I'm fifty?
How I don't want them to judge me,
But myself do, when I see through their insecurities.

Isn't it weird that I have a bad memory,
But keeps remembering a long back embarrassing scenery?
How I can't remember my real laugh,
But smile more when I feel like crying.

Isn't it weird that I want to be good at everything,
But am nothing but a fully flawed human being?
How I tell people to talk their problems out,
But am myself afraid to cry out loud.

Isn't it just so weird that I'm tired and bored of living,
But am just too afraid of dying…?

Alter Ego

Bhakti Barad

I want to be seen,
I want to be heard,
I want to be well read with books
On my shelf I bought as a teenager, which
Has not yet finished…
I want to file my grandparents' pictures to
Remember the day they fought on their
Way to honeymoon.
I want to be dressed in chic and plaid skirts
With my bare skin showing, without the
Fear of strange hands.

I want to speak aloud; not just words.
But with angst, my emotions slamming
The poetry I wrote.
I want to learn new words,
Words that I found magical, philosophical and
Historical with power,
I want to sink into the arms of that fictional boy,
Whom I thought is real when I dreamt of him.

Disarrayed

I want to find him, find him in someone else…
I want to reach out to people's hands to
Save myself from falls rushing down my throat.

I want to be intelligent, to
Speak hours of lecture to satisfy myself.
I want to learn physics and math and
Also how the earth moves.
I want to watch classic movies to
Imagine myself in a new setting every day, to
Find an escape from the harsh realities.
I want to be the male lead to
Walk like an iron and to
Keep mum, whenever I feel like crying.

I want to be forrest gump.
I want to fit in, especially
In the party of people where stories are
Made and destroyed,
Where love is found and lost,
Where hands are held at night
Beneath the blanket,
Want to fit into instances where
Glasses are poured over intellect, instead of ice!
Fit into the world of dark academia and poetry,

Fit into my mother's jeans as well.
I want to love the freckle in his finger,
If he allows me to,
I want to be pretty as Rose in Titanic.
I want to be chosen to be
Kept forever in small fragile glass case,
Like a rose in the museum of their eyes.
I want to be held tight with
Everything he owns from palms,
Eyes, jackets and even words,
I want to smell like a candle from the medieval times,
With lavender essence and innocence,
I want to be brave like the people
Battling puzzles in their minds.

Stuck in a Loop

Bhuvi Gupta

Will I ever be free?
In this web of lies,
Will I ever find me?

Like the sky full of
Birds flying with glee,
Will I ever be free?

It eats me inside out
Like a pest.
This ugly thing rooted
Deep in the chest.

It doesn't let me eat,
Sleep or even dress.
Always plotting against me
Like in a game of chess.

Unfortunate

Hema S

Unfortunately,
Distressed voyages have
Found a way to
Exert its influence.

Sometimes, the
Encircling darkness can't
Be distanced from me
Or I'm unable to challenge it.

The most valuable novelty
Can't be embraced at times,
As the waves of my psyche
Have lost their rhythmic movement.

Moreover, a framework of delightful
Hopes can't be represented,
As the external disturbances
Have gained their ultimate triumph.

Unfortunately,
It's an extended tussle to
Manage an exceptional routine
And balance my everyday working equations.

Her Verse

Srishti Karkara

She has scars
Which she carries with pride,
She fears
But she doesn't fear doing,
She doesn't fear being 'her'.

She cries,
She doubts
But she still fights
And she still believes.
Because she knows
There is nobody for her,
Unless she, herself stands up for her.

There is so much of her she is yet to see,

There is some spark in her she is yet to unveil.

She will slow down,

But she will go on

And she will sing her verse,

Which will be louder than the noise around her.

And the most beautiful thing about her,

She will be silent through it all,

She will smile through it all.

Time Passed By

Jagruthi Kommuri

In the blink of an eye,
Time passed by.
Left clueless of why or what am I.
I think I'm going to try and try.

They say, time once gone,
Never comes back.
But can we face the past,
If it plans to attack?

They say, now or never
And do or die.
But we set alarms for future,
Then is it not a lie?

No matter happy or sad,
Seasons passed by
Like a winged hourglass
Depicting, how time flies!

It never stopped before,
It won't stop now.
May be, just maybe,
The answers are in the 'how'.

You and I may remain the same,
Or we may likely start to change.
Just in a moment, life's a different game,
Because time passed by and we can't rearrange.

My Reflection

Srishti Karkara

I am just shattered pieces of glass,
I can't put it back together as it was.
But, this time
I will use the same pieces and arrange
Them in a new and beautiful way,
So I can always know that
Even after all the falls,
This arranged version of mine is also mine.
I am not the same as I was,
Just trying to be better,
Just trying to look at myself in the mirror,
One more time.

Lost and Lonely

Keertika Shivee

Crying feels like a burden,
A weight that just gets heavy,
No amount of silence works,
No sound makes you free,
The thoughts in the head always swirling,
The emotions distorted and weary,
Some sheds them once and feel like living,
Some till the soul wants to be buried.

The hiccups start later some time,
As if begging you to stop thinking,
Hoping you would feel the pain under your eyes,
The burning has started it seems,
But as time passes and loneliness hits,
You have gone so far into yourself by tearing,
That the scars of heart start hurting,
And your body starts aching.

But it is the end of it that is worrying,
The point where you sit and stare at nothing,
The point where everything is numbing,
Only the tears, you and your shattering,
No voice, or vision, or thoughts, or breathing,
Just a heart and its tired beating,
Just another night of silent screaming,
Another night of defeated self,
Another cry,
Of the lost and lonely.

For Myself

Reeba John

I have never felt this lost, like I feel today.
This much darkness was never in my life.
Like every other kid who had grown up to
Believe in magic, in miracles and in dreams,
I too grew big, old enough to believe
In goodness, in virtuousness and
In humanity.
I had a strong conviction that
Truth always triumphs and
People who are honest will be admired.

Little did I know that one day,
I will lose my faith in all
The goodness I had stood for.
I never knew truth can hurt me more than
The way lie could ever do.
I am now aware that there is no secured path
And everyone who smiles with us
Is not actually with us.
They change so quickly, I thought.
They may have their reasons, their priorities.

On a fine Sunday morning, it hit me.
The realization came as the high tide
Of the lunar day.
I barely slept with all the pain
Lingering in my chest, which
Slowly crawled to
Each and every inch of my body,
Making me a dumb and a weak creature!
The agony I suffered due to the betrayal of
My loved ones was incomparable.

I could not just put it into words,
I just know I was not better than
Any paper tore, crumbled down and stomped off.
My eyes were never dry,
My smile never came back.
Once and for ever, I became a whole other person.
I became an arrogant one for many and
Selfish for others, while I was striving
Hard to put myself together.
Really struggling hard to stand still
And defend myself.

The ones whom I had thought as mine,
Did not actually care for me and
All along, they looked for a
Chance to overthrow me.
It was my big mistake to trust them blindly that
I failed to notice their double faces.

But do you know, "what's best?"
I am now aware of their true faces, which
They can never hide from me anymore.
It makes me more privileged over them.
Now I am back in my control that
I won't trust anyone blindly.

Though it was aching to master the lesson,
I am not bragging...Trust me, I am a fast learner.
I learned and evolved so fast.
Nothing comes in my way anymore.

The Great One

Halo Golwin

"Wah… My project didn't make it to the Science Fair again!"

As I wept, sparks of gold and silver flicker across My eyes. I felt something bouncing on My shoulder repeatedly, while potato chips were being crushed on My other shoulder, sending shockwaves throughout My room. It was then Teddy, Polar and I fully entered a dream, bound by nothing in the real world except My brilliance…

Polar may be puny but his words were sharp. He viewed everyone with contempt except the Great One. Teddy was just Polar's opposite. He was plump but encouraged humility in the Great One. As long as I had them, I would always reign supreme across the realms of visual arts, music, project work and academics.

My first performance in Visual Arts was smooth sailing. Upon sensing My immense potential, My teacher coaxed Me to design a symbol for the seminar. Wow! Another mundane event involving thousands of students… Convincing the Principal and the Head of the Department that My design was flawless proved easy. With My divine powers, I could seamlessly become one with the symbol and infiltrate the social conscience. Everyone would be subconsciously thinking about Me. With My clairvoyance, I easily foresaw that My symbol would be engraved into a glasswork souvenir given by My school to a renowned minister of Singapore. Alas! My symbol was overshadowed by a song composed by My arch nemesis, Chester. Even Gods have limits. My school Principal erroneously claimed that Chester had created an "entirely new culture" with his musical masterpiece.

"You're letting the opinions of others get to you! Everyone must bow down to you and you only! All hail the Great One!" Polar comforted Me, placing his furry paws on My hand.

"No Polar, Golwin shouldn't dismiss the opinions of others to make friends," Teddy retorted agitatedly. I fiddled with Teddy's arms, trying to soothe his nerves as he spoke.

My two soft toys were the only ones who understood My inner conflicts, unlike My parents and friends who simply dismiss them due to their feeble minds.

"Whatever, I have innumerable strengths in academics and piano anyway! I will always triumph because I'm the one and only!" I mediated. As part of My determination to rule over every field known to mankind, I made preparations to bamboozle My piano examiner with extensive repertoire and solid musical knowledge that I had possessed. I will unquestionably win a Grammy for this!

Upon gracing the examination room, I saw Teddy and Polar sitting on top of the piano, having a heated discussion. Teddy began: "If the arrow of time points in only one direction that means mistakes are inevitable. Doesn't that mean that nobody can be *Perfect*?"

Polar replied: "Golwin is *Perfect* to me even with his *Imperfections.* His mistakes are imperceptible to begin with. He would easily bamboozle his examiner and get a distinction." My fingers fumbled clumsily across the piano as Teddy's and Polar's discussion distracted me. "You two... Keep it down! Can't you see the Great One is playing his magnum opus?" I screamed at them. Upon My outburst, the examiner looked at Me, as if I were a lunatic.

"What's the cadence?" the examiner tested Me.

"*Im-Perfect* cadence!" I replied confidently. What a piece of cake! He should have tested Me on *Perfect* cadences since I was *Perfect* to begin with.

Upon completing My grand finale, I glanced at the examiner expecting him to be dumbfounded. The horrors! He only congratulated Me for completing the examination. Worse still, he accused Me of being nervous throughout the performance. It seemed like I won't be getting My Grammy award soon.

It hurts! It hurts! How My heart breaks!

"Wah..." My floodgates burst, drowning the entirety of Singapore in eternal misery. I better wipe away My tears on the way back to school. I can't let them see Me like this. "Maybe the examiner is just envious and throwing shade at you!" Polar exclaimed earnestly, staring unblinkingly at Me with his hypnotizing eyes.

"Just forget it. Your mistakes are permanent, but you might still get a distinction," Teddy reasoned, patting Me on the back.

Unsurprisingly, My piano teacher broke the much belated news that I had secured a distinction in the examination. "Well, better now than never," I starkly remarked to Teddy and Polar.

"It's a travesty that you didn't get a Grammy instead! You were *Perfect*!" Polar quipped. "No Golwin, you should be satisfied," Teddy mumbled.

While My visual arts and music performances were ongoing, I also had to confront My most troublesome performance, the project work, in order to reach *Perfection* that I rightfully deserved.

Wow, I had to deal with actual people! Against our will, we were quarantined into a group of six, including Teddy and Polar. My group decided to address the socio-economic challenges faced by Syrian refugees in Malmö, Sweden under the theme of "Crisis". However, the larger existential crisis was the fact that Teddy and

Polar had to work together…

"Golwin! You're better than all those peasants combined! You're just too kind and not asserting your dominance over the rest!" Polar asserted, making an adorable "plop" sound every time he bounced on My head.

Teddy fervently disagreed: "Nonsense! It's wiser to work together with your teammates." "Maybe I would let them do more work. They should be grateful that they have Me in their team. They're going to get easy tasks because of Me anyway," I exclaimed, with Polar nodding in agreement.

However, as I analyzed them more closely, they could perhaps surpass Me. Person A had every leadership quality you could imagine, especially humility. Person B was exceptional in designing PowerPoint slides for our flimsy strategies. But worst of all, Person C had the audacity to imagine a sports strategy to unite refugees and Swedish youths, that would only lead to disaster without My intellect.

Much to Polar's disgruntlement, he plucked out his fur in anger while Teddy attempted to give Me a thumbs-up. Sadly, Teddy had no fingers. Nonetheless, I gave him a fist bump instead!

Before we knew it, the results had arrived. All six of us clinched an A for Project Work, while the rest of My class was ruthlessly butchered with Bs. I tried to use My powers as the Great One, but I couldn't rewrite their horrific fates. What's the point of being *Perfect* if I can't use My powers to make others *Perfect*? It was then My mortality began to strike Me…

I finally met My match with My most arduous performance, despite Polar's disagreement. As expected, I passed the aptitude tests for two prestigious universities, granting Me the opportunity to do research projects at their campuses.

"Golwin is the embodiment of *Perfection*! One day, Golwin will undoubtedly take over the entire NUS and NTU with his brilliance," luminous stars twinkled in Polar's marble-like eyes.

"Well, he worked really hard on this. He even forgot to bathe for months! He barely even brushed his teeth! Gross!" Teddy grimaced. After returning home, I started reading highly advanced topics while scrubbing Teddy and Polar for the first time in months. Teddy cajoled Me to work harder, while Polar rolled his eyes believing that hard work was beneath Me.

My professor even gave Me a PhD thesis to read. I was aghast as the ostentatious vocabulary in the thesis was incomprehensible, even for the Great One. Cracks momentarily appeared in My bears' marble-like eyes as it was beyond anything we had ever encountered. It was not long before I had to present My proposal for My research project. My professor heralded in countless Professors working in diverse fields all around the globe to watch what was potentially My first downfall in life. Come what may, let the show begin!

Polar watched in anticipation, as he attempted in vain to find a seat that fit his minuscule size. Teddy sneered at his nemesis, as he comfortably sat on a seat. As the performance had begun, Polar attempted to squeeze into Teddy's seat. Teddy reluctantly gave in. Throughout My horrific performance where I desperately referred to My slides to find coherent words to say, Polar just ate his popcorn noisily, while Teddy crushed potato chips in his mouth, sending shockwaves throughout the theatre. Oh wait, neither of them had mouths! They were just crushing food mindlessly against their faces! Both of their noses and mouths were greasy and oily. Disgusting! Looks like I have to wash them again after this saga ends.

One of the professors dared to question the Great One: "Do you know what an atomic defect is?"

"Oh, that's easy! It's a missing atom that used to be at a lattice site," I humbly replied.

"Correct! It's a dislodged atom," the professor reaffirmed Me.

Wow! This professor's brain must be dislodged to ask such a question that was beneath Me. "Oh, his hard work paid off," Teddy remarked, looking to Polar condescendingly, while Polar attempted to avoid his gaze.

"So, what would you do for your novel research?" the professor enquired further, scheming to disgrace Me.

"I… I think I plan to substitute the bismuth-site and iron-site cations with other cations? I'm not sure if this affects the properties..." I replied unconvincingly.

For the first time, Polar was speechless and muttered: "But… but… Golwin was supposed to be the Great One…"

"This is all because you kept spoiling Golwin, Polar," Teddy remarked carelessly, not realizing Polar was on the verge of tears and had dropped his popcorn on Teddy's scarf. After the conference ended, I broke into tears for the second time, embracing Teddy and Polar's fur which had turned greasy from the food. The water flow from My tear ducts was so turbulent that it washed away the grease off their fur entirely, making them squeaky-clean again. Maybe I'm not as godlike as I had thought. Will the show be able to go on?

Time flew in a *Perfect* linear fashion, blatantly ignoring My emotions. Even the Great One couldn't control the flow of time. Before I knew it, I was cutting My fingers due to My *Perfect* coordination in using diamond cutters to cut glass substrates. Blood oozed out of Me. Maybe I wasn't immortal after all, for blood was a sign of mortality. It was then I realized that I want to see My research paper published in international scientific journals more than anything, even My own life…

I attempted to stop the bleeding as Teddy and Polar cuddled it with their fur. It was one of the rare times where both of them were in harmony. As they attempted to overcome this bloody crisis, Polar asked Teddy to get first aid.

“No Polar, did you forget we’re not real?” Teddy reminded.

At that moment Teddy and Polar glitched ever so slightly, I sensed something wrong, but I was in too much agony to pay heed to it.

I started to ignore all the voices around Me. Moving on to the synthesis of nanofilms! Wait, where are they? I fumbled around nervously, desperately searching for the nanofilms that I took one whole month to work on. Someone must have stolen them! Are they trying to steal My glory?

After painstakingly reconstructing new nanofilms from scratch, I realized that they were dead to begin with! No photocurrent detected at all! I tried endlessly to get the nanofilms to produce results, but everything ended up in vain. Even if there was a light at the end of the tunnel, it could just be a train menacingly racing to smack me down!

As Polar finally began to see My flaws, he lamented, “You lied to me the whole time, Golwin. You were everything I wanted to be.”

“Failure is a norm in the academic world. A failed experiment is not at all a failed life,” Teddy comforted Me. The light was slowly fading from Teddy and Polar’s eyes. It was then that Polar collapsed in Teddy’s arms, as he started to glitch continuously.

Upon noticing My dismal outlook, My professor attached a layer of aluminium foil to the surface of the nanofilms and connected the electrodes.

Let there be light: and there was light. Yet, darkness engulfed me, swallowing me whole. Something snapped in me as I realized I would be nothing without my professor, who solved my problem instantly.

“The nanofilms are revived! That means we can publish the results in international scientific journals! Golwin, aren’t you happy?” my professor exclaimed.

I smiled in response to hide my pain for the first time.

In the visual arts, nobody came to see my performance. In music, I was never confident in my performance. In project work, I couldn't perfect the performance of others. In research, I failed to perform to the perfect standards of my professor. I was never special to begin with, as my successes were always contingent on the actions of those around me. This was who I am: someone pretending to be someone I'm not.

Upon my realization, I noticed that Teddy and Polar were becoming increasingly translucent. "It seems like our time is almost up. It was fun being with you, Golwin."

"Yeah, it was so wonderful."

Wait, is this for real? My soft toys sound as if they are saying their final goodbyes to me! Aren't goodbyes supposed to be sweet? Why do they sound so excruciating now? No, don't go! Don't leave me alone! Who's going to accompany me in my darkest moments? Who's going to cheer me up when I'm sad? I still have so many moments that I want to spend an eternity with, together with Teddy and Polar!

Still shaken by my disillusionment, Polar smiled at me and said his final words: "You were perfect to me, Golwin." As I hugged Polar for the last time, he vanished completely. "I'm not." I choked out the words bitterly, still smiling in pain. There was a sour aftertaste in my mouth, but I knew that it wasn't from my addiction of sniffing acetone in the lab all day.

Teddy looked up at me peacefully, knowing that his time was also up. "Maybe one day, you will find someone who can make you smile for real..." Teddy slowly vanished, leaving a smell of popcorn. I tried to hug Teddy for the last time, but he disappeared before I could.

It was then the magical reality I had built so painstakingly collapsed. Polar symbolized my yearning to be unique, while Teddy symbolized my yearning to connect with people. How can they form twin reflections of my true self, when they weren't real to begin with? It was time that I embrace my illusions and rediscover the true essence of who I was meant to be.

The Rain That Never Ceased

Sanay Shah

The rain poured incessantly, its huge droplets thudding on the tarmac. The dismal sky mirrored the city's dreary tone, imparting a melancholic pallor to all it had touched. People hustled through the rain, heads down, seeking refuge from the never-ending torrent. One of them was Garj.

Garj endured through the pools of water. His steps heavy and sluggish, as if each step held the weight of a million broken aspirations. His garments were wet to the bone and stuck to his skin. He had always been an emotional man, someone who felt intensely and cared excessively. It was both a blessing and a curse, since with every high came a low and he found himself in the depths of despair. He was trapped. He had recalled a day when the sun sparkled exquisitely, and excitement filled the air. He was a wealthy businessman with a loving wife and two adorable children. They lived in a lovely house on the outskirts of town, and their days were full of love and fulfillment. But fate had other ideas for him, as it usually has.

It started with an unexpected economic collapse, sweeping through the country like a hurricane, leaving destruction in its wake. Garj's once-thriving firm seemed upon the verge of bankruptcy. The weight of debt tipped the scales on him, consuming the life, out of his aspirations. He laboured furiously to save everything he could. But the harder he struggled, the deeper he sank.

As the rain poured down, Garj found himself standing in front of a dilapidated building that housed his former office. The sight of it offered him a mixed feeling of frustration, hopelessness, and remorse. He pulled open the creaky door and entered. The musty odour of wetness welcomed him like an old friend. The walls were covered with fading images, which were glimpses of the happy times when success was just around the corner. The memories returned back to his memory with each step. The sound of co-workers laughing, phones ringing, and discrete discussions over deals…But now all that was left was a hollow shell—a relic of what had been. All the memories he had created within those walls still persisted, plaguing his thoughts like a ghostly apparition.

Garj proceeded into his former office, where he had spent endless hours pouring through data, making call after call, and building his empire. He sat behind his battered desk. His fingertips traced the wood's grooves. The weight of his failures weighed heavily on him, almost crushing him.

Outside, the rain resumed its relentless assault. The sound seemed to be a never-ending reminder of his predicament. Garj gazed out the window, watching the water run down through the glass. His eyes swelled up with unshed tears. He very well knew the reality that he had been avoiding. His life was finished. A bolt of lightning struck the area, throwing spooky shadows on the walls. Garj's attention was drawn to the worn-out leather suitcase on the floor, which had been neglected and abandoned. He leaned down and opened it slowly, revealing a collection of letters. Each letter was stained with the tears of his broken aspirations.

The weight of his emotions got heavier as he had read through the letters. Regret swept over him like a tidal wave, threatening to drown him. He'd lost everything—his business, his house, and his family. Outside, the rain appeared to mirror his sadness, as if the sky had mourned for him.

Garj rose up. The weight of his dilemma was bearing down on his shoulders. A never-ending symphony of sadness hammered at the glass. Even though it felt impossible, he understood what he had to do. He needed to find a way out of this darkness to seek reparation and to reconstruct what had been destroyed.

Garj closed the briefcase and walked out of his previous workplace, leaving the ghosts of his past behind. The rain pummelled down, drenching him to the bone. Yet, he remained unafraid. He inhaled deeply, savouring the uncertainty that lay ahead. The emotions that had characterized his life would no longer confine him. He'd climb above them, even if it meant forging his own path through the darkness. Garj went into the flood. Each of his step was determined enough to ignite a flickering flame in the darkness. The rain continued to pour. The drops wiped away the traces of his prior life.

The world was a blank canvas waiting to be painted over. Garj believed he had the fortitude to face whatever that lay ahead and as he vanished into the rain-soaked streets, his narrative hung in the air like an ending awaiting its conclusion.

Only, time would tell if Garj could break free from the anguish that had shackled him and if he could summon the strength to rebuild his life from the ashes. The rain persisted in its downpour, reminding him of the trials and tribulations that were ahead. And in the distance, a glimmer of hope awaited, a little light that refused to go out.

The Shadow of the Flame

Kai Jennings

People say nothing hurts worse than death, but they clearly haven't forced themselves to stop loving someone because that person didn't love them anymore. Especially, when that someone was their parents... When I was eleven, Covid decided to make its first appearance. It was the big killer pandemic that stopped you from meeting your friends and loved ones. It was the big killer plague that forced you to confine into the four walls of your house and to spend time with your parents. It was the big killer plague that forced you to see a novel horrifying version of parents as well.

Now, I know a lot of people would say, "Kai it isn't fair, they are just stressed!" That was what I told myself, except while using my dead name because at that time, I hadn't seen myself truly. I used to tell them exactly the same thing through tears. I would choke on, that it was stress...

Now I'm guessing you want to pause here, thinking I got a detail wrong, but absolutely no. As an eleven-year-old, who didn't have much acquaintance with the foul language, clearly knew what stress was.

They used me as a punching bag, and I realized that punches on the back hurt less than that I felt in my heart. So, I turned back to it and try to put aside my pain. I put my earphones, connected it to a laptop as old as I was and drowned myself in music. I had read a lot of books, and I stopped here for some reason, as I am half way through the *Order of the Phoenix* by J.K Rowling. It had too much of an info dump in the wrong place I guess, but I picked the first book up and read the series from start to finish.

I guess if you're reading this, you know that when you read, there is this hunger in you—the need to feel normal, to feel like the so called "actual" person.

I've had that hunger since I was small, and I read *Bambi.* I was insatiable. I went from *Bambi* to Enid Blyton and to Harry Potter. Unfortunately the hunger was not at all gone when I was done with Harry Potter, I hadn't laughed. So, I went to my sister and asked her for a book I had heard her talk of, *Percy Jackson.*

Percy Jackson made me feel like a real person, I laughed and cried and laughed again. It was so enthralling. After I had done with it, the hunger only got worse and to keep it at bay, I start reading other books. Otherwise, the reality would come rushing back so that I read and read, even during my online classes, when I was used to be asleep and even while brushing my teeth. Unfortunately, my parents had caught me reading when I was supposed to pay attention to classes, and they took away all my books. But I had hidden my kindle. Of course, I was too scared to take it out and ended up in great misery.

At that time, I got reconnect with my old school friends. I didn't have a phone of my own. So, I used my mother's web WhatsApp. We talked and I was feeling good. I also felt real. That is until my Mom told me to not talk to them anymore since we were talking about school and how it was an absolute shithole. Turned out, she had been reading my chats.

I felt like I had no privacy so that I stopped talking to them. I got depressed to the point where I wouldn't eat, and I could barely breathe. There was one book left in the home-library, which is just placed in a hollow space under the TV, *The Diary of Anne Frank.* I started reading it and it was good, but I couldn't enjoy it because it made me feel that was breaching someone else's privacy. I know she was no longer alive, but it wasn't right. So I put it down and never picked it up again.

Only when you lose something, you realize its true value. So I had nothing to do but focus on myself. So, I started watching movies and rereading books online. I came across a word beyond my stock of vocabulary, 'gay'. I found more out about the community and finally came to the serious realization that I fit in it.

For a year or so, I switched between 'gay' and 'bi'. Then when I decided who I was, a lesbian gender entered the chat. Through a lot of struggle I have now found out myself as a trans and boyflux, where I am on the male gender spectrum, but my gender fluctuates between he/they, they/them, and he/him pronouns. And I am pan, asexual and grayromantic, having romantic attraction much less than other people do. Along with this I also found out that my parents were homophobic. Now, if you ever see me, you'll say," Yeah he looks gay." My parents also thought the same and the pain got even worse.

When you have an infected leg which doesn't heal, you have to cut it off. When you have so many people, whom you adore as your dear loving ones and who don't love you, just cut them off. I'm fourteen and I started writing now, just to let people who have had similar experiences, to know that they're not alone. If you ever feel lonely just reach out to me, I will respond and listen to your sorrows, that the so called "actual human beings" are not yet ready to pay attention to. I'm just fourteen and haven't recovered at all. To those who feel the same and encounter the same struggles, I wish you all the best and hope that you are doing okay. If you ever need someone to talk to, I'm here… Here, always!!!

Stepping Out

Anna Reji

"Step out Vibha!" This was not a new thing which Vibha heard from the people around her. She knew she had to step out of her comfort zone to grow. 'Exposure', they called it. People believed that she lack exposure. Yes... she was not exposed to the outside world as children of her age were.

Vibha was a shy child, and no one cared to correct her. People around her expected that she would have soon altered herself in the process of growing up. No one saw the pain in her eyes when her math teacher had scolded her for scoring less in a class test and also the teacher didn't care to ask her why. The scoldings she received were dramatic monologues, not conversations with her teachers which would have helped Vibha to reveal that her mother was not at home to help her learn the sums. She yearns to be asked about it but it didn't happen. If asked, she would have revealed that her mother had a night shift in the previous night of the last test.

Vibha was forced to occupy the last row in her kindergarten dance performance because she was shy. And as always, no one asked her why couldn't she perform well when she stands in the first row. People called it a silly thing which deserves no importance in their decisions and plans for her future. When I used the collective noun 'people', remember that it excludes her mother. Her mother was the only person who always stood by her side. "Amma"- the woman she had hated in her childhood and teenage days, but whom she began to adore as a grown-up.

Vibha was expected to be enrolled in an entrance coaching institute when she passed the class XII board exams with 89.80%. Although she had remained silent all these years and when the question of what she wanted to become arises, she broke her silence and expressed her desire to study English Language and literature. She knew very clearly that she could not be able to become a good teacher, but she had immense faith in her ability for creative writing. When she joined an aided college in Kerala to pursue her degree and again in another one for her post-graduation, the so-called 'people' around her came back, with the topic of lack of 'exposure' in the colleges in Kerala.

Today when Vibha stands as a post graduate in English Language and Literature, she knows very clearly what to do next as she has encountered and get inspired by so many 'people' who trusted Vibha more than they trust themselves. Oh! This time there is a slight change in the meaning of 'people'. This time 'people' includes both her parents. She struggled really hard to earn the support of her father, but finally, she succeeds!

The Story Behind the Sad Eyes

Kai Jennings

When she was younger she often dreamed of fairy tales, she dreamed she would find love with the most wonderful person in the world. And as she got older, she would read fiction. But it all changed when she turned eleven. She no longer dreamed of finding love, instead, she was tormented by nightmares of pain.

She read as Covid came, attended zoom calls for school and looked happy and bubbly all the time, just like a normal eleven-year-old. But her eyes were sad. She drowned herself in the world of books and tried not to breathe, not to float up, but she always did and when she did, she was miserable again.

She eventually stopped paying attention to classes and started watching videos on YouTube, watched movies, and even played games online. But as time passed, she became more aware. One day, when she woke up and as she listened to Taylor Swift, re-reading her favorite book, she realized it... She liked girls. Later it would be a great joy, but at that moment it only increased her sadness. The feeling of oppression, the feeling that she couldn't talk to anybody haunted her.

Every night her parents dragged her to their room, locking the door behind them and every day she would beg for death. They would say the most vile things, unimaginable to their own child, telling her that she was a disappointment, screaming that they wish she wasn't born. She wept and blamed Covid as the reason for their anger and stress. But eventually, she broke. It was too much for an eleven-year-old.

When she was twelve, she dove into the world of books, running away from reality as if her life depended on it.

Her parents asked her if someone had touched her, and she denied it disgustedly. Disgusted that they couldn't see what they were doing to her. Disgusted that they couldn't even bear to accept it. They had ripped her heart out.

She would forget what they said later though, but the feeling haunted her worst nightmares and every waking moment. She was never going to be the same again.

Death Knocked on My Door

Srishti Sareen

What if a human is formed into their true form once they experience all their death rites? What is that waits ahead for them? Is it a vicious cycle or a turmoil that they have to face until they die to undergo, until they are released from the vastness of sadness? Do humans work like clocks? Or like Earth which follows the same orbital path, until a year passes by and repeats the same. Never stop at all. How would one feel to resurrect from one's own ashen form? Or how can it be possible to live behind the closed doors, like a puppet? Or holding on to the last silver thread of something passionate, just like that of a memory, a piece of art, or the last video you recorded of them. However, it is nothing, but a bundle of illusions all wrapped up with a knot. Will it all vanish when they will be burned, buried, or casketed all over again?

How does it feel to have that experience whether someone is dead or alive? It is difficult to live every day; waking up and feeling that gut-wrenching ache to bleed a little—to feel something human. The humanity is something that had already lost. It is painful to have memories and people will surely be in utter chaos and confusion, whenever they come to know their exact time to bid farewell to everything. To be human and be stuck in a loop that one cannot outrun is really exhausting. And in that exhaustion, one can feel their blood thicken and not be able to do what the body is supposed to do. That's what life is. Truly, a fragment of nothingness behind forged names: the plausible notes you want to leave after your suicide. In total, it is the horrifying pretexts along with the name of death that scare us to not die. It makes us feel something out there awaiting us. But one could write countless suicide notes, until they snap, and emotions spill out like a glass of red wine on a beautiful white rug. Maybe it won't hurt. Not long enough. Because there won't be a chivalrous knight, in shining armour on the door step all the time. Because, death could also knock on the door, right?

In the fleeting dreams of reality, people find an escape in a land, where souls don't bother each other. It's a world where no one is forced to live a pseudo–life. It's obviously something far beyond the heartaches caused by human interactions. No one talks or texts. They not even check on their neighbors, whether they are dead or alive until there is an unbearable stench. At that very point, the senses kick in. One discovers the truth behind closed doors. Because before all that, it was inhumanity, that holds onto the meat suit, like a parasite way too hard. It's the land that breathes in the silences and human discontent. So is it necessary? Probably, yes. Will it work? No one knows. But until then, people have lived in a world where they are dead, way before they ever took birth to live on that land- a land of witchcraft and the unrealities of humans. So, let it be real even if it is masked or too scary to be real.

Somehow the things that exist far beyond the human touches are what let them live an extra year, with just the hope of attainment or to see the lucid appearance of redemption. Even if it is not so true, let it be unrealistically real. Not for them but for the land to prosper. It is flawed and unhinged to believe in a world where nothing hurts because it will surely be loveless. A world where silences grow deeper: silver threads are in a tight knot for everyone and everything, just to stay intact. Maybe that's what it is to have people around. A world where wishes come true according to one's own needs. To feel how it is to have a hummingbird's heart. Or sleep and softly die.

Wake up and follow the same routine until something feels not broken anymore. Because now it is fragmented so many times that the pain has dissolved itself in the void of nothingness. Will it hurt to feel choked? Undoubtedly yes. But can there ever be a way out of it? May be or not. Until then, live in the silences. Die a million times and again one more time. Learn words that are far beyond the limits of a dictionary...A land where death is prominent and necessary just to make us feel human again. And once through all the satanic rituals, one is back to square one. To live a life like a human, they will surely cross the horizon and reach a standstill where they will have to die until it doesn't hurt all over again. So let it happen. Bleed until your body is bloodless and crisp enough to burn under the sun to be dust again.

Slice of Shattered Thoughts

Binta Elsa Biju

To have a serene and peaceful mind seems to be a 'forbidden fruit' in today's world. Everything is dynamic, even the relationships God has gifted us since birth. The novel ways in which people perceive reality have brought about drastic changes, almost in all realms of human life. In modern world, everything and everyone are attributed with new meanings and identities; thereby deconstructing the barriers of a prescribed framework. Mind, the receptacle of diverse emotions is now brimming with fruitless and irritating thoughts. It often murmurs to detach from the worldly pleasures and pressures to have a better understanding of true 'Self'.

Whenever mind gets shrouded with dark haunting thoughts and passions, a vision of the so called 'Self,' embracing tranquillity and peace always serve as a succour to move on. Some experiences we encounter in this unpredictable and unrelenting journey are inexplicable. Sometimes, words seem to fail in expressing the intensity of emotions that overpower us at certain points. Harsh realities offered by life are at times, capable of making us insane. This insanity has the power to take us to an illusionary state by shattering the cocoon of reality. Don't limit ourselves to fit into a structured framework prescribed by the society. Follow our hearts so that we will be followed by others in future.

Don't be submissive to the pseudo, outdated norms and notions that still manipulate lots of minds. Let the message of love, care and respect be heard everywhere. Life is all about one thing—survival. When life situations shower thousand questions of negativity, face them with a positive smile and move on. Trust thyself... The best is yet to be!

Featuring the Co-Authors

Halo Golwin

The Halo is not merely a symbol, but an epithet for Golwin's whimsical friend who inspired him to exercise freedom through writing. His works often accentuate the absurd in what's mundane, while amplifying what's insane. For all avid lovers of art and poetry, do visit @not_a_blank_slate_anymore on Instagram!

Hema S

Hema S is an Assistant Professor in the PG Department of English at Yuvakshetra Institute of Management Studies, Palakkad. She has published several of her poems in various anthologies and journals, by various publishers in India. She is also the author of multiple research essays on literary topics in various journals.

Anna Reji

Anna Reji is a post-graduate student of English Language and Literature at Mar Thoma College, Thiruvalla. She is a genuine lover of literature and spends her time in reading and writing. She dreams of pursuing a career in teaching and works hard to achieve her dreams. She loves listening to music as well. By becoming a contributor to the anthology, "Disarrayed", she hopes that her identity as a budding writer will eventually bloom!

Srishti Kala

Srishti embarked on her academic journey with English literature at Delhi University before taking a bold leap to the USA, where she delved into the realm of Biochemistry—a field seemingly at odds with her previous studies. Presently, she is dedicated to her pursuit of a doctoral degree in Biochemistry and molecular medicine. Beyond her lab endeavors, she finds solace in pampering her two beloved fluffy companions at home.

Keertika Shivee

Keertika says that she exists but isn't breathing. Is that even existing? She says she is like the chilly breeze before thundering rain in winters, withering in the in-betweens, as if she only comes to shake the world when the world tries to bury her and fails, just enough to let it know that even without existing she commands the universe. Is that what is called existing?

Alen Tharakan

Alen Tharakan is an M.A. English student of Mar Thoma College Tiruvalla, Kerala. His notable achievement is securing an A grade in AIFEST International Poetry Competition 2023. His hobbies are reading and singing. His personal goal is to write a Gothic novel.

Srishti Karkara

Srishti Karkara is a 17-year-old student studying at Tagore International School. Writing is not only a hobby for her but also a tool that has helped her to express her emotions and her true self; she posts poetry on Instagram (@nsstofsk) with the purpose of touching hearts!

Bhavika Gupta

Bhavika Gupta, a high school senior, seeks solace in books, writing, singing, and her quiet reveries. In the midst of a busy crowd, she remains an ardent bookworm, finding comfort in a cozy corner. Through the intricacy of her narratives, she aims to interlace her thoughts harmoniously, in a rhythmic and captivating manner.

Jagruthi Kommuri

Jagruthi is a simple girl, who believes that words resonate like beautiful melodies within the hearts of readers. She's an MBA post-graduate and currently working as an HR Associate Analyst. Her poetic journey had begun during her B.Com graduation and she discovered that each carefully chosen word has the power to ignite hope in the minds of her readers. To her, words are akin to musical notes and through her verses, she strives to reveal the essence of life, like enchanting songs that touch the soul.

Divvya Gupta

Divvya Gupta is a Chartered Accountant by profession but what truly makes her special is her love of weaving words with emotions and giving them an unmissable rhythm. She sees herself as a faineant poet who believes that her words can create magic and make society a better place to live in. She endorses the thought that if she can lead to any betterment of the society through her words, it will be her way of paying back to the amazing world we all dwell in. She seeks support from all her readers and encourages honest feedback on her work. Feel free to reach out to her on: cadivvyagupta@gmail.com

Juwel Zacharia

Juwel Zacharia, hailing from the scenic landscapes of Kottayam district in Kerala, is a post graduate in English Literature. She illuminates young minds as an English teacher, infusing her classroom with a fervour for verse. Beyond the chalk and blackboard, her creative spirit resonates with life's subtleties; crafting verses that unlock uncharted depths of human emotions and connections. She firmly believes in poetry's transformative power to heal, inspire, and kindle conversations that traverse borders and cultures.

Ananya Singh

Ananya Singh is a budding writer, who loves to create stories. Using simple yet powerful words, she shares emotions through her writings. With each tale, she learns and grows, excited to bring imagination to life.

Praneel Dev

"Words are our more inexhaustible source of magic."—Albus Dumbledore. The author is a firm believer in the strength and magnificence of books, writing and literature. He prefers to spend his time delving into new worlds and losing himself in fantasy.

Amiteshwar Singh

Introducing Amiteshwar Singh, a serene and cheerful soul with a penchant for poetic expression. A devoted aficionado of mysteries, he finds solace in penning verses that explore the enigmatic corners of life. With over 30 heartfelt poems to his credit, Amiteshwar continues to weave his lyrical magic, sharing his creations on his social media handle @shayarjasoos. Drawing inspiration from unconventional topics and personal experiences, his verses offer a unique perspective that resonates with readers far and wide.

Susmin Eapen

Susmin Eapen is a young literary enthusiast, who is presently working in the medical sector. She completed her Doctor of Pharmacy from Pushpagiri College of Pharmacy, Thiruvalla, Kerala. She had done her schooling in Merryland Kindergarten and St. Joseph's School, Abu Dhabi. She is very much into music and reading.

Khushi Shukla

She is a curious and artful individual with a passion for exploring new ideas, currently a second-year student pursuing B.Tech CSE. With a diverse skill set spanning coding, dancing, sketching, writing, music, and badminton, she is ambitious to make a meaningful influence on the world at large.

Reeba John

Reeba John has a postgraduate degree in English Language and Literature and is currently a teacher trainee with a strong enthusiasm for reading, composing poetry and exploring the fascinating world of letters. She is a committed and responsible individual who aspires to support productive ideas and deeds as she pursues her goals.

Bhuvi Gupta

Bhuvi is a young and energetic girl with a passion to learn anything and everything. This quality helps her to venture all the possibilities to explore new dimensions of herself. She is good at expressing her feelings and thoughts into words.

Gauri Agarwal

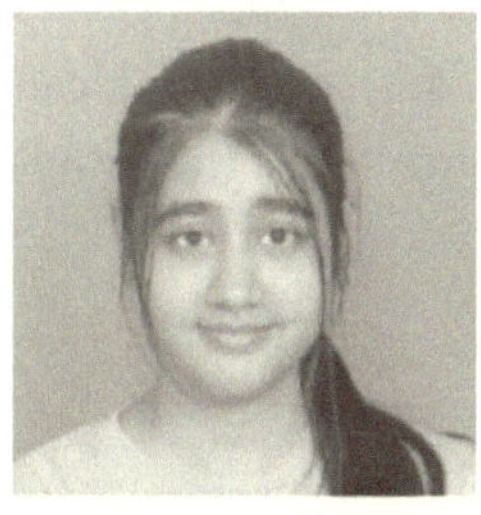

Gauri Agarwal is just a 17-year-old, who has just started her new journey with new people at a new place. She writes or tries to write whatever that helps her communicate with herself better. Before, she used to think of writing as something just for fun, but these days she has started exploring herself more and writing has become something more than she just enjoys doing. She likes creating things any drawing or DIY, though she is not very good at it. She also likes to read or watch things that make her think a lot in depth.

Anju Elizabeth Kurien

Anju Elizabeth Kurien, an admirer of art who seeks self-expression through her drawings and words. The world of pencils, pens and blank papers is her asylum. Most of her writings accompany her drawings, posted in social media platforms. She has penned several poems like Healing, Unrequited, Numb and many other pieces of writings which lack proper title. She aspires to create works of art to which her audience could easily connect, yet with deeper layers of meaning.

Varnika Sasi Magesh

Varnika Sasi Magesh is based in Chennai and is currently pursuing her Bachelor's degree in Computer Science and Engineering from Coimbatore Institute of Technology. She's always had an eye for impactful write-ups, and she often delved into the world of letters that drove her to put her thoughts together using words. She draws most of her inspiration from the film, "Dead Poets Society", which has influenced a lot to romanticize the things in her life.

Swastika Bhattacharyya

Originating from a city adorned with lush greenery and subsequently transitioning herself to an entirely novel setting, Swastika's journey was etched by both the crucible of hardship and allure of nature itself. The vast cerulean skies, distant lands, serene lakes, and the kaleidoscope of her native traditions profoundly captivated her imagination and ignited her with a sense of wonder. Infused with an unwavering optimism, she expresses her essence through the medium of words, pen and paper, vivid canvases adorned with colors and the cadence of rhythms. Her affection for classical rhythms finds expression in her passion for dance. Apart from this she has let her voice to various anthologies and graced the digital galleries of Instagram .Beyond her realm of creative pursuits, she embraces athleticism and seeks out adventures as a means to witness the world's inherent beauty. She firmly holds the belief that in order to achieve equilibrium in life, one must harmonize with something that resonates deeply within. For Swastika, this is a philosophy she feels, she's discovered through intricate weaving of words, forming enchanting tapestries that have the power to touch people's hearts effortlessly.

Bhakti Barad

Bhakti is a psychology major and psycho in nature. She is very creative in her words and the way she pours out her entangled mind on paper is like a single thread. She loves watching true crime documentaries, which do not match with her empathetic nature. Her quirkiness stems from how basic she can be and her ironically stupid jokes will definitely bring out a disgusted chuckle from the people around her. She is the personification of her poems and her art, without which she would not feel alive or would have been a brain eating zombie.

Srishti Sareen

Srishti Sareen was born and brought up in Ludhiana. She completed her Bachelor's in Commerce and is now pursuing her Masters in English. She started writing in 2016. Ever since, she has not stopped her passion for words. Reading and writing are like a drug to her. She is passionate about embracing old songs and ghazals. All these tiny moments she has with things she loves are what make her happier.

Asad Chaugule

Asad is an Automotive Surface designer by profession. Along with an interest in sketching cars, he has a flair for writing poems in English/Urdu and goes by the pen name of Assad Omar. Asad loves exploring nature to enhance his creative skills in designing and writing.

Sanay Shah

Sanay Shah is a 17-year-old student from Mumbai. He nurtures a fervent love for writing and is a dedicated literary enthusiast. Alongside his pursuits in football and economics, he aspires to weave stories that readers can resonate with, carving his path as a celebrated author in the times to come.

Rhythmi Rosa S.

Rhythmi Rosa S. is a poet from India. She completed B.Com and works at an MNC now. She writes poetry, articles, quotes, and short stories. She creates literature in motivational, nature-based, social, commerce-based themes. Her literary works are published online and also in few poetry anthologies. Her motive in writing poetry is to create valuable literature for the readers.

www.inkfeathers.com

We love creating beautiful books for you!

Come be a part of our ever-growing community of authors.
Grow, write, and publish with us!

Connect with us on socials.
We'd love to hear from you!

@Inkfeathers Publishing

www.ingramcontent.com/pod-product-compliance
Lightning Source LLC
LaVergne TN
LVHW091032150826
845672LV00006BA/1780